HIGH SCHOOL MUSICAL 3 SENIOR YEAR

WILDCATS FOREVER

Adapted by Lara Bergen

Based on the screenplay written by Peter Barsocchini

Based on characters created by Peter Barsocchini

Executive Producer Kenny Ortega

Produced by Bill Borden and Barry Rosenbush

Directed by Kenny Ortega

DISNEP PRESS

New York

D0009568g

First Edition

1 3 5 7 9 10 8 6 4 2

Library of Congress Control Number: 2008903898

ISBN 978-1-4231-1207-5

For more Disney Press fun, visit www.disneybooks.com
Visit disney.com/HSM3

Senior year. It was finally here! And once again the East High Wildcats were high school basketball champs!

To celebrate, Troy Bolton hosted a huge party in his backyard. Everyone was having a great time—especially Gabriella Montez and Taylor McKessie!

Even the head coach of the University of Albuquerque's basketball team came to the party!

"We're counting on seeing you both in Redhawk uniforms next season, right?" he asked Troy and team co-captain Chad Danforth.

"Done deal," said Chad, giving Troy a high five.

But Troy was uncertain about his future, and where to attend college.

Gabriella wasn't so sure about next year, either. She had already been accepted to Stanford University—but it was a thousand miles away!

Gabriella felt so at home at East High. Why, she wondered, did everything have to change so fast?

CHAPTER 2

Work on the spring musical began the very next day.

"It's about all of you," Ms. Darbus, the drama teacher, explained. "We'll call it *Senior Year*," she said.

At first, some of the seniors said they didn't want to participate. There was too much to do before graduation! But Gabriella convinced everyone to do it. After all, it would be the last time they would be able to share the stage together.

Now it was time to think about the prom!
Troy hadn't officially asked Gabriella to go
with him yet. But she was hoping that he
would. And he did on East High's rooftop
later that day.

"Is that a yes?" Troy asked Gabriella as
they danced in the rain.

Gabriella smiled back at Troy. "In every
language," she replied.

Their friend, Zeke Baylor, was getting ready to ask Sharpay Evans to the prom. But as it turned out, he didn't even officially have to ask her.

"Oh, Zeke, glad you stopped by," Sharpay said. "You're taking me to prom. Dance lessons begin Monday. Questions? No? Good. Toodles." Then she waved him away.

Chad wanted to ask Taylor. But it wasn't easy for him. Troy helped him by replacing his basketball with a bouquet of flowers. Then he sent Chad over to Taylor's table in the cafeteria.

"Taylor McKessie . . . *please* be my date to the senior prom!" Chad yelled nervously.

Taylor thought for a moment. "I'd be honored," she replied.

Soon everything was settled. Everyone had a prom date. And everyone had a part in the spring musical.

Then Gabriella got another letter from Stanford University. She was more confused than ever.

CHAPTER 3

Stanford had offered Gabriella a place in their freshman honors program. And she didn't know if she should go.

"You should be throwing a party, not keeping it a secret," Taylor said.

"But the program starts at Stanford next week! I'll miss everything," Gabriella said sadly.

"You'll come back for prom and graduation," Taylor told her.

Gabriella wanted to stay at East High, and she almost did. But then she talked to Troy.

"Of course you should do the honors program," he told her.

He knew Gabriella wanted senior year to go more slowly. But they were going to graduate, and there was no way to stop it.

"I get it," she said with a sigh. "It's senior year and this is what happens."

Gabriella decided to go to Stanford and come back for the prom and for graduation. She wished senior year could be half as easy for her as it seemed to be for Troy. She was having trouble accepting that pretty soon she would be leaving East High for good. She would just have to make the best of it.

But with Gabriella gone, nothing was the same. East High felt empty. And the spring musical was almost about to fall apart. Troy couldn't wait for Gabriella to come back for the prom.

Then, two days before the prom, Troy got
a phone call. It was Gabriella.

"I've run out of good-byes, Troy," she told
him. "I'm sorry." It had taken Gabriella two
weeks to get used to being away from Troy
and all her friends, and she just didn't think
she could go back and then leave again.

Troy couldn't believe it. And neither could Chad.

"Hey . . . that's lousy, man," Chad said. But soon they would all be moving on.

"We're at U of A; it's a whole new ball game," he told Troy.

"Maybe I don't see my life as a 'ball game' anymore," Troy replied. Maybe, he thought, everything *didn't* have to change, after all.

CHAPTER 4

Two days later, the East High prom was held as planned. The girls wore their prettiest dresses. The boys wore tuxedos and bow ties. The gym looked amazing, and everyone danced all night. Everyone, that is, but Troy and Gabriella.

Gabriella spotted Troy on the Stanford campus dressed in his tuxedo. "I don't believe this!" she exclaimed. "But prom is . . . tonight—in Albuquerque," she said.

"My prom is wherever you are," he replied.
"And if I'm going to have a last dance at East
High, it's going to be with you." Together they
waltzed around the quad.

Then Troy told Gabriella how much East High had changed since she'd left.

"You may be ready to say good-bye to East High," he told her, "but East High isn't ready to say good-bye to you."

Deep down, Gabriella knew she wasn't ready to leave East High for good just yet. If they hurried, she thought they might even be able to get back to East High in time to participate in the spring musical!

CHAPTER 5

Troy and Gabriella arrived at East High just in time to save the show from certain disaster. Not only was the cast lost without Troy and Gabriella, but their understudies were in big trouble!

Troy's understudy was Wildcat-in-training Jimmie "the Rocket" Zara. While he was pretty good with a basketball, he'd never been in a musical before. Even worse, Sharpay, Gabriella's understudy, was allergic to Jimmie's cologne!

Still, Sharpay didn't know which was more horrifying, sneezing her way offstage or watching Gabriella and Troy save the day.

"Perfect, go for it," Sharpay told them in defeat.

But then Sharpay had an idea. She would reclaim her role in the show and play herself. She wasn't going to let her understudy, Tiara Gold, stand in her way! The girls decided to battle it out onstage, in true divalike fashion.

After the musical ended, Ms. Darbus announced where the seniors would be attending college. When she finished reading off everyone's name, she turned to look at Troy.

"And now, a senior who I believe has a decision to make—Mr. Troy Bolton. Troy?" Ms. Darbus asked.

Troy had made a decision that surprised everyone. He wanted more choices next year, not fewer, so he had decided to go to the University of California in Berkeley. It offered him both basketball and theater . . . and it was exactly 32.7 miles away from Stanford, *and* Gabriella.

Graduation had come just as quickly as everyone had feared. But it had also brought the East High Wildcats together . . . all except for Chad, that is. He was nowhere to be found. Where was he? they all wondered.

Troy hurried to the gym—where, sure enough, he found Chad. He was shooting hoops, like always. Maybe he wasn't as eager to start something new as he'd once said . . . especially now that Troy was going to a different school.

"So I guess when they hand us the diploma . . . we're actually done here," he said to Troy. "One question. Does Berkeley play . . ."

"Yep." Troy hurried to answer him. Their two basketball teams would be playing each other in November!

Yes, the East High seniors were going on to new things . . . but that didn't mean they had to forget where they'd come from. After all, as Troy told his classmates, East High wasn't just the place where they had gone to school.

East High was a place where teachers such as Ms. Darbus helped them be whoever they wanted to be. It was a place where coaches such as Troy's dad taught them how to be part of a team. It was a place where a person such as Gabriella could make a whole school better. And it was a place where they could build friendships that would last forever.

"Once a Wildcat, always a Wildcat!" Troy cheered.